MW00981277

Gribich™ And Friends
POOF WOLF'S NEW HOUSE

Written by **Marcus Porus, Shirley Porus**
and **Philip Lange**

Illustrated by **Steven Jay Porus**

Copyright © 1996 Doog Publishing Group
Gribich and all other characters are © and TM 1996 Steven Jay Porus
All Rights Reserved.
No part of this publication may be reproduced in whole or in part, or stored
in a retrieval system, or transmitted in any form or by any means, electronic,
mechanical, photocopying, recording, or otherwise,
without written permission from the publisher, with the exception of
a brief quotation included in a review.

Library of Congress catalog card number: 95-92693
ISBN: 0-9646125-2-6

First Printing June 1996
10 9 8 7 6 5 4 3 2 1

[1. Childrens–Fiction 2. Space Travel–Fiction 3. Animals–Fiction]

This book is environmentally friendly.

Printed on recycled paper utilizing soy based inks.
Printed in the United States of America.

"Gribich and his friends teach such wonderful lessons to children in such an entertaining fashion. The books are exciting, well written and beautifully illustrated. However, equally as important, they give the children role models to follow and morals to learn. This is just the kind of book that we in education love to use with our children in discussions and in conflict resolution. I am looking forward to additions to this series."

Sharon J. Haddy, Principal
Norco Elementary School
Norco, California

A little red ball with bright yellow lights raced to Earth. Inside was a plump and happy visitor from the Planet Doog. Gribich was his name. He was excited that he was going to see his friends again. Gribich smiled to himself. He was almost there! He could see his friends below.

Deep in the forest, Bobbin Robin chirped, "I can fly higher than you can jump, Cabot!"

Poof Wolf boasted, "That's nothing. I can lift Burl higher than you can fly, Bobbin!"

Cabot Rabbit shouted, "Poof, I double dare you to climb that tree." Burl Squirrel was there, cracking nuts with his teeth. He was too busy to respond to all the chatter.

The spaceship glided down
without a sound. It landed in
the clearing. Gribich jumped
out. He went into the forest
to surprise his friends.

"Hello-o-o, Hello-o-o everyone. Did you miss me?" Gribich asked.

Everyone stopped what they were doing. "Gribich, you're back," Bobbin cried. "Of course we missed you!"

Burl raced down the tree to join the others and said, "I'll bet Gribich can fly higher than anyone!" He chuckled and added, "Unless you have spaceships I don't know about." Everyone laughed.

Suddenly, Poof stopped laughing. He sensed that something was about to happen. The air was still. The leaves on the trees didn't even move. "Something is wrong. I can feel it," Poof said.

Bobbin agreed. "I feel it too. What's happening?"

Cabot and Poof began to sniff the air. They looked worried. Just then, Gribich's spaceship started BEEEEEPING, BEEEEEEPING louder and louder! Then, there was a low, rumbling sound coming from underground. The ground shook. The trees in the forest swayed back and forth. The animals were scared.

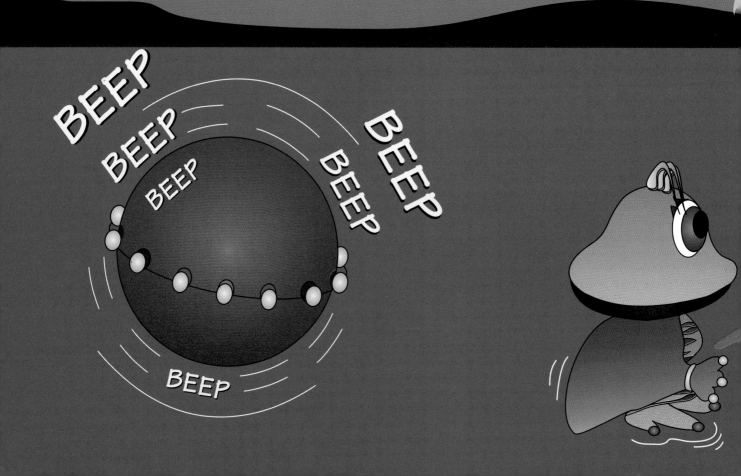

Gribich shouted, "Hurry, hurry everyone! Stay clear of the trees! Try to hide from anything that might fall on you."

They searched, but couldn't find
cover. So they ran toward the
clearing where it would be
safer. They could hear
trees falling behind
them. CRACKLE,
SWOOSH, BANG!
They didn't look
back and just
kept running!
Finally, they made
it to the clearing.
They waited there
until the earth
stopped rocking and
rumbling. It was over!

Swoosh

BANG!

Crack

Bobbin peeped,
"I'm so frightened."

Burl stuttered,
"I've never felt
anything like
that before."

"Don't be scared. We're all OK,
aren't we?" Cabot said calmly.

Gribich added, "No one was hurt
because we moved quickly. We
did the right thing."

Poof was still panting. He asked, "What was that?"

"That was an earthquake," Gribich explained. "It was caused by underground rocks knocking and rubbing against each other."

Bobbin cried, "Why did this happen? What did we do wrong? Was it because we bragged to each other?"

"You didn't do anything wrong," Gribich said softly. "Sometimes earthquakes just happen."

Burl asked, "What do we
do if it happens again?"

Cabot answered,
"The same as
we did today!"

"That's right!"
Gribich added.

Burl was anxious to see if their homes were OK. He said, "Come on, let's start with Bobbin's nest." When they got there, they saw everything was fine. Bobbin chirped with joy. They were all happy for her.

Next they went to check Cabot and Burl's homes. Happily, everything was OK there too. Poof's house was the last one they had to look at. They moved ahead with high hopes.

When they saw Poof's cave in
the mountains, everyone
became silent. Many rocks had
rolled down the mountainside.
A very large rock had landed
right in front of Poof's doorway.
He couldn't get inside.

"What am I going to do?" Poof cried.
"Where am I going to sleep tonight?"

Gribich answered, "Don't worry Poof.
We'll all help you rebuild your house."

Burl, Bobbin and Cabot looked at each other. Burl asked, "What can we do? We only know how to build homes for ourselves. We don't know how to build a home for a wolf."

"We'll learn together," Gribich replied.

Bobbin snapped, "What's the use. It will fall down if we have another earthquake."

"No. We're going to make it stronger," replied Gribich. "I know we can do it!" Everyone felt encouraged and ready to start.

"First we must remove the big rock from the opening," Gribich explained. "We'll need a large, strong branch to roll it away."

"That's easy," chirped Bobbin. "I'll fly above the forest and look for one."

Before long, she spotted a very large fallen branch. Bobbin flew back and guided Burl and Cabot to it. They gathered all their strength and lifted the branch into the wagon.

"Whew," Burl sighed.
"That was real heavy."

Cabot agreed. After resting, they started back to Poof's house. They huffed and puffed all the way, pulling the wagon.

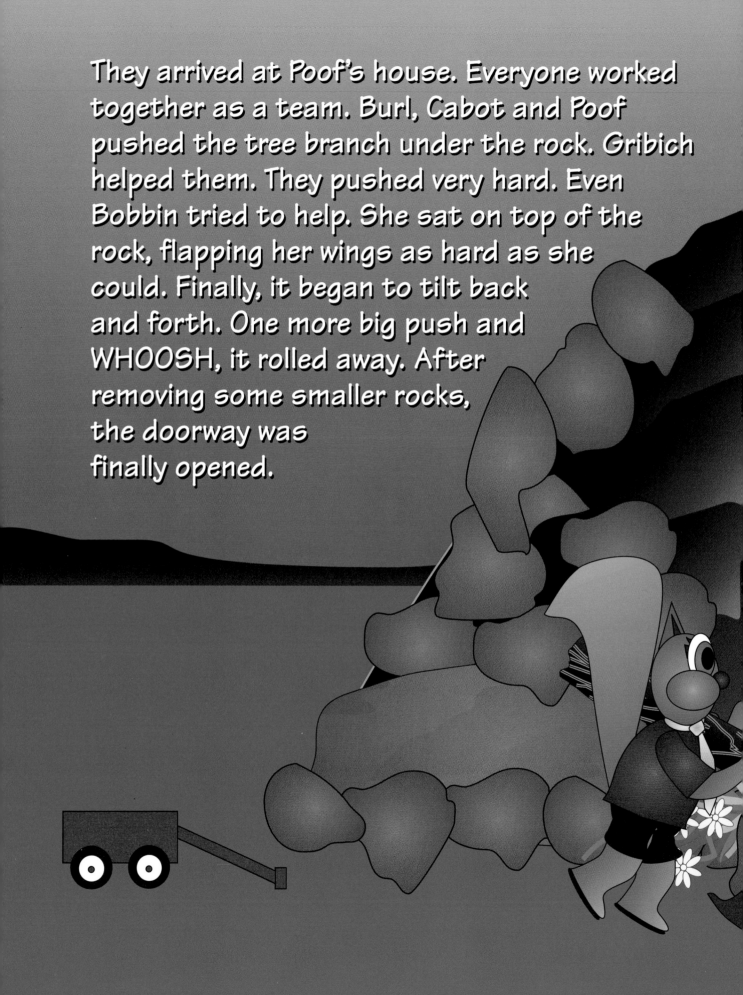

They arrived at Poof's house. Everyone worked together as a team. Burl, Cabot and Poof pushed the tree branch under the rock. Gribich helped them. They pushed very hard. Even Bobbin tried to help. She sat on top of the rock, flapping her wings as hard as she could. Finally, it began to tilt back and forth. One more big push and WHOOSH, it rolled away. After removing some smaller rocks, the doorway was finally opened.

Looking inside, they could see more small rocks. Together they lifted them into Cabot's wagon. The cave was finally cleared. Gribich said, "We can build a wood frame around the opening. This will make Poof's home stronger and safer."

"Oooh, I like that idea," Poof said smiling.

Cabot hopped up and down. "Let's get started. We want Poof to have a safe home by tonight."

The animals went to look for more wood. There were some big branches close to Poof's house. They carried them back in the wagon. Cabot and Burl cut and shaped the wood with their sharp teeth.

When they were finished, Poof helped Gribich put the frame together. Bobbin gathered dried grass and twigs for inside of Poof's house. She wanted to do something extra special for him.

After a few hours they were finally done. Poof looked at his new house and said, "WOW, this is really great! Thanks everyone.

Bobbin, thanks for making the inside of my house so comfortable. I can't wait to sleep here!" They were all happy for him.

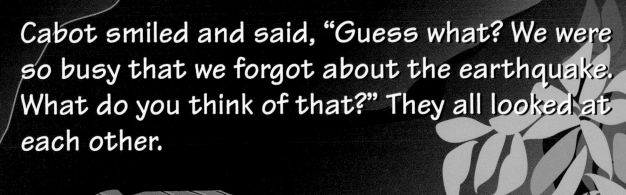

Cabot smiled and said, "Guess what? We were so busy that we forgot about the earthquake. What do you think of that?" They all looked at each other.

"GEE, you're right," said Burl. "Now we know what to do in case there's another one."

Bobbin chirped, "Three cheers for us!"

Gribich was ready to go to his spaceship. They all walked to the clearing with him. Poof said, "Thanks for everything, Gribich. We learned so much today."

"I did too," Gribich said.

The animals waved good-bye as Gribich climbed into his spaceship. He waved back and before they knew it, he was gone. They felt so lucky to have him for a friend.

The End? No Way!

We would like to acknowledge
Corinne Bergstrom
for her editorial direction.